This Book Belongs to

A Gift from Woodworkers for Children Charity

D1450698

For Hal, Leo, Ruby, and Siwan

ATHENEUM BOOKS FOR YOUNG READERS
An imprint of Simon & Schuster Children's Publishing Division
1230 Avenue of the Americas, New York, New York 10020
Copyright © 2012 by Alan Snow
All rights reserved, including the right of reproduction in whole or in part in any form.
ATHENEUM BOOKS FOR YOUNG READERS is a registered trademark of Simon & Schuster, Inc.
Atheneum logo is a trademark of Simon & Schuster, Inc.
For information about special discounts for bulk purchases, please contact Simon & Schuster Special Sales at 1-866-506-1949
or business@simonandschuster.com.
The Simon & Schuster Speakers Bureau can bring authors to your live event. For more information or to book an event, contact
the Simon & Schuster Speakers Bureau at 1-866-248-3049 or visit our website at www.simonspeakers.com.
The text for this book is set in Hank BT.
The illustrations for this book are rendered in pen and ink and computer colorization.
Manufactured in China
1212 SCS
First US Edition 2013
2 4 6 8 10 9 7 5 3 1
CIP data for this book is available from the Library of Congress.
ISBN 978-1-4424-8294-4

How Dinosaurs Really Work!

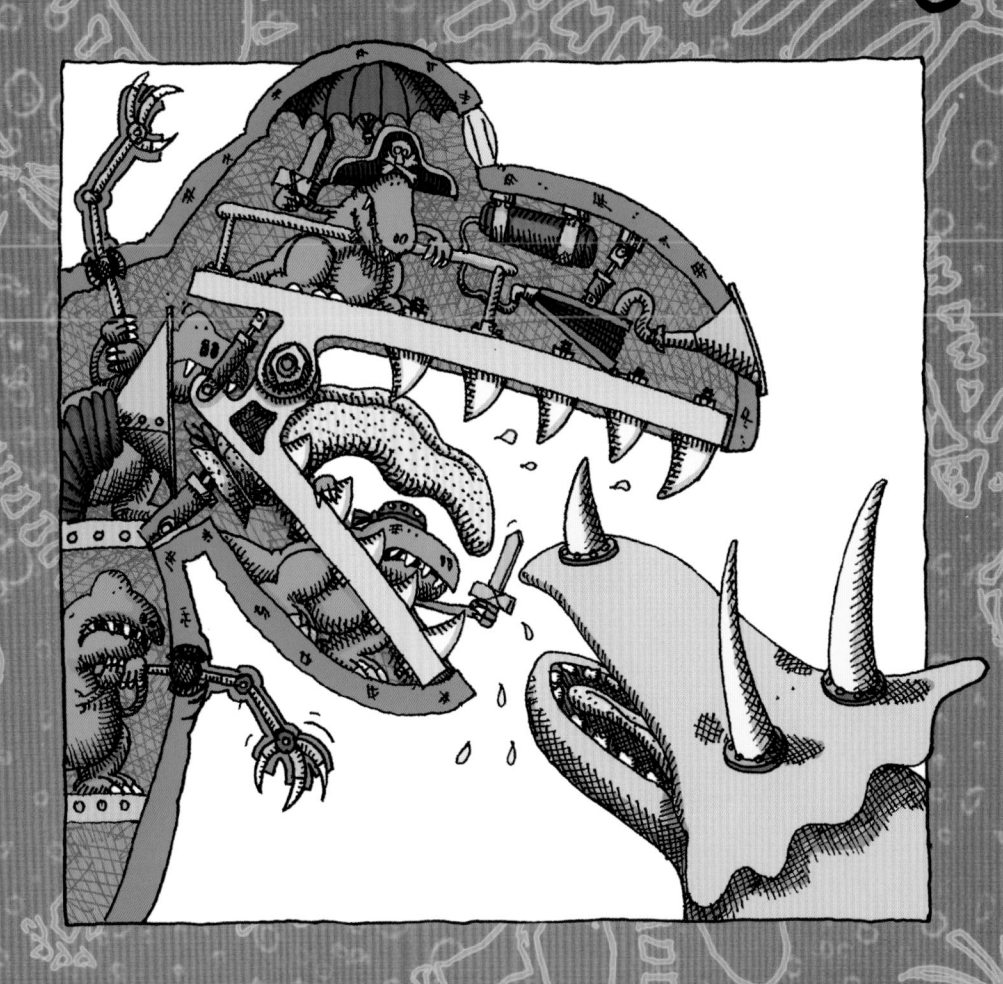

by Alan Snow

atheneum

ATHENEUM BOOKS FOR YOUNG READERS
London New York Sydney Toronto New Delhi

THE TERRIBLE LIZARDS!
Or not . . .

Are you our cousin?

There was a time long ago when dinosaurs ruled the Earth. The word DINOSAUR comes from two Greek words: DEINOS, which means terrible, powerful, or wondrous, and SAUROS, which means lizard . . . so they could be called TERRIBLE LIZARDS . . . except that, in fact, not all were terrible and none were lizards.

You see, these prehistoric reptiles were beasts of many shapes, sizes, and types, and they were more closely related to modern birds than lizards. Some were meat-eating monsters; others were plant-eating creatures.

Triassic Period
250–204 million years ago

Jurassic Period
204–143 million years ago

Cretaceous Perio
143–65 million years ag

Terrible vegetarian dinosaurs attacking prehistoric giant carrots (which probably didn't exist).

Dinosaurs didn't exist when your parents were young, so attacks on the way to school were not a problem.

QUICK!

So when DID dinosaurs rule the Earth? Well, you know that your parents are old—dinosaurs are much, MUCH older than them. Even when your grandparents were young, there were no dinosaurs. The first dinosaurs appeared about 230 million years ago, and all the dinosaurs died out around 65 million years ago.

Humans have only been around for about 200,000 years.

I love cutting lines!

Uh, I was here first.

Tertiary Period
64–1.8 million years ago

Hey, you guys! Try a burger!

Dinosaurs lived on the planet for about 165 million years (which is about 800 times longer than us humans have been here).

Our ideas of what dinosaurs looked like come mostly from fossils. These were made when dead dinosaurs became trapped in mud and were slowly buried. Over time the soft parts rotted away, but the bones turned to stone.

When early fossils were discovered, people often didn't know which part of the dinosaur they had found. One man thought he had found a horn from a dinosaur's nose—but he had actually found its thumb!

He's heavy! We've used ten tons of clay already!

This one would have made a good pet.

Help! I'm sinking.

Hold on! We'll get you out.

People began to study dinosaur fossils and imagine how the complete creature would look. Today paleontologists (people who study fossils and the nature of dinosaurs) spend a lot of time modeling dinosaurs on computers, trying to work out how they would have looked and even moved.

Dinosaur fossils are very rare, so we may never know the shapes and types of ALL dinosaurs. We also don't know what color dinosaurs were; they might have needed camouflage to hide or markings to attract a mate—or even to scare off other dinosaurs!

STEGOSAURUS (STEG-uh-SAWR-us)

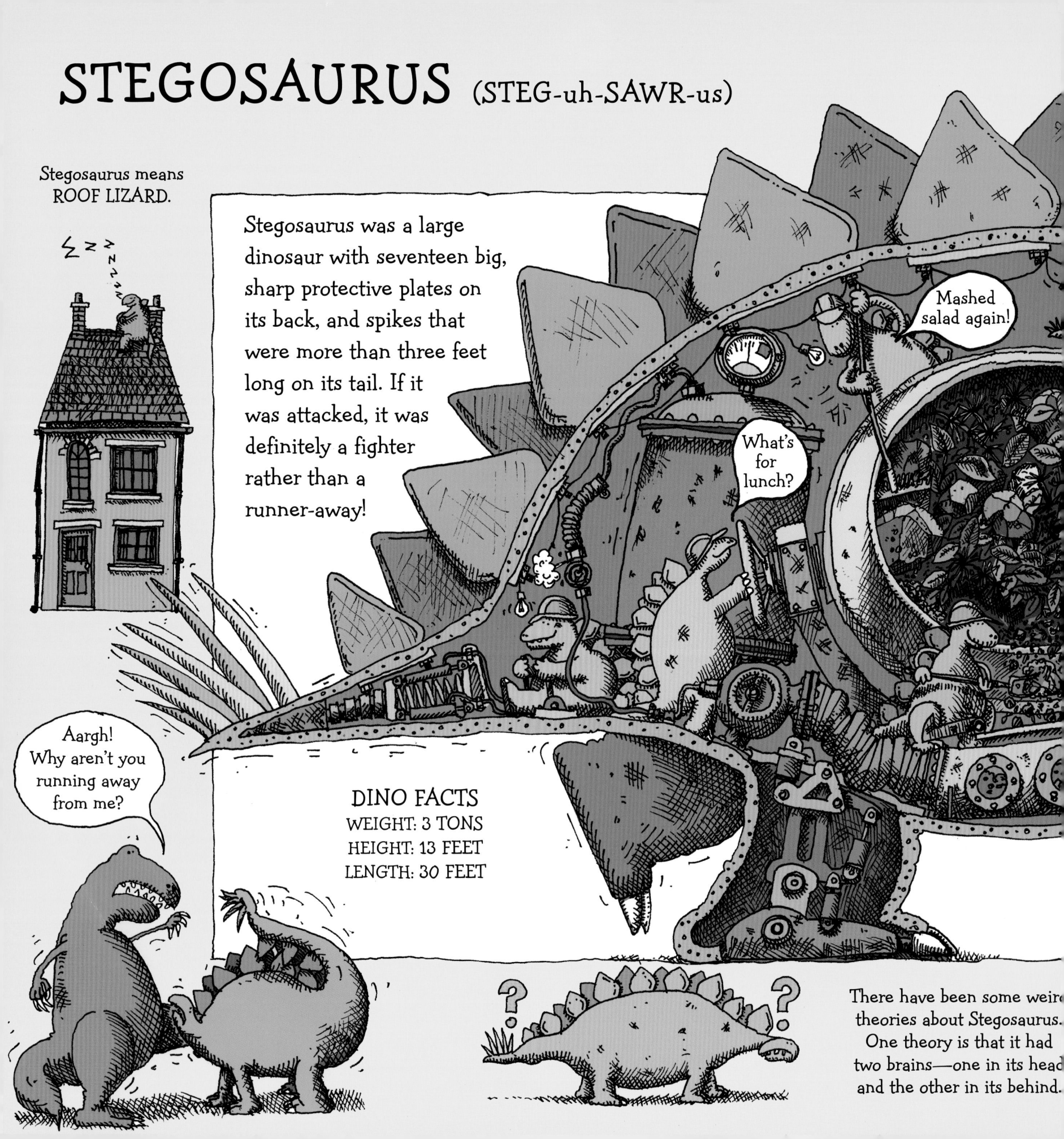

Stegosaurus means ROOF LIZARD.

Stegosaurus was a large dinosaur with seventeen big, sharp protective plates on its back, and spikes that were more than three feet long on its tail. If it was attacked, it was definitely a fighter rather than a runner-away!

Mashed salad again!

What's for lunch?

Aargh! Why aren't you running away from me?

DINO FACTS
WEIGHT: 3 TONS
HEIGHT: 13 FEET
LENGTH: 30 FEET

There have been some weird theories about Stegosaurus. One theory is that it had two brains—one in its head and the other in its behind.

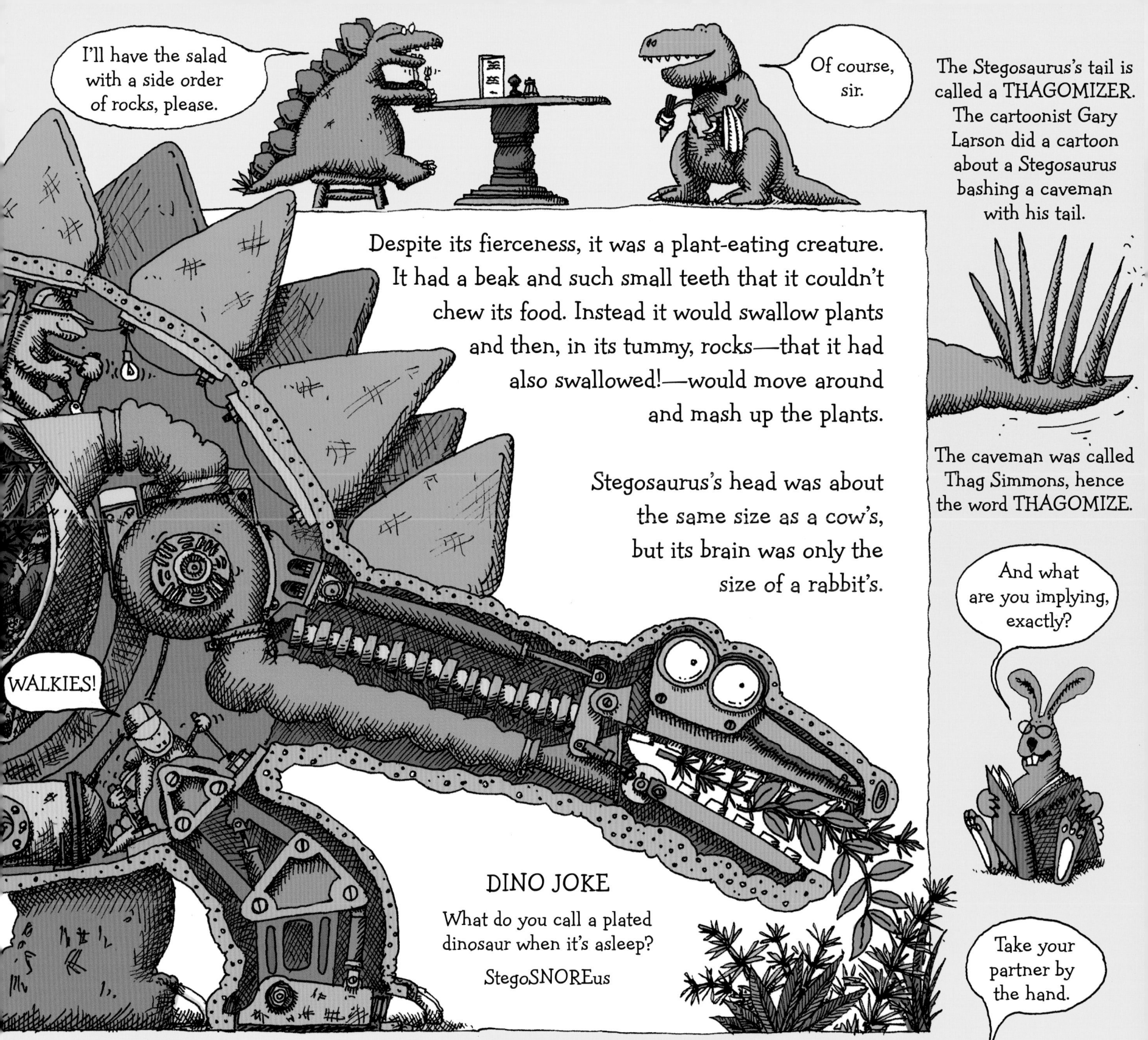

I'll have the salad with a side order of rocks, please.

Of course, sir.

The *Stegosaurus*'s tail is called a THAGOMIZER. The cartoonist Gary Larson did a cartoon about a *Stegosaurus* bashing a caveman with his tail.

Despite its fierceness, it was a plant-eating creature. It had a beak and such small teeth that it couldn't chew its food. Instead it would swallow plants and then, in its tummy, rocks—that it had also swallowed!—would move around and mash up the plants.

Stegosaurus's head was about the same size as a cow's, but its brain was only the size of a rabbit's.

The caveman was called Thag Simmons, hence the word THAGOMIZE.

And what are you implying, exactly?

WALKIES!

DINO JOKE

What do you call a plated dinosaur when it's asleep?

StegoSNOREus

Take your partner by the hand.

Another Stegosaurus theory is that it walked on two legs.

TRICERATOPS (try-SAIR-uh-tops)

Triceratops means THREE-HORNED FACE.

Triceratops was a three-horned dinosaur with a huge protective plate over its head. It had one of the largest skulls of any land-dwelling animal. Triceratops used its head to defend itself, as well as to attract mates. Its head may even have helped it to keep cool! Despite having this protective armor, its skull may have been too delicate for it to charge at other dinosaurs.

Triceratops lived at the same time as Tyrannosaurus Rex, but it wasn't as bright. In fact, it wasn't even as bright as a crocodile.

DINO FACTS
WEIGHT: 8 TONS
HEIGHT: 10 FEET
LENGTH: 30 FEET

Triceratops ate ferns and other low-growing plants.

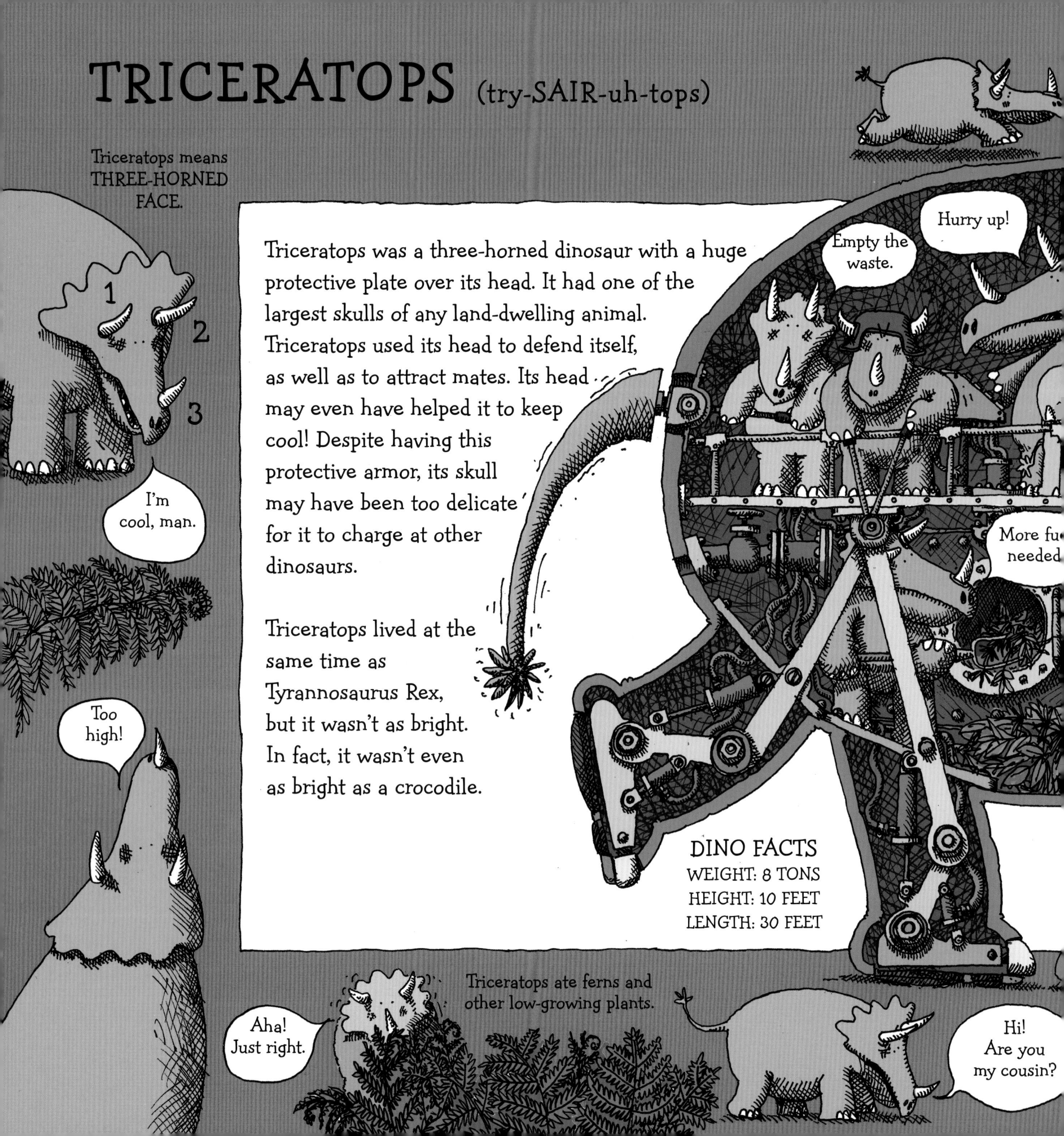

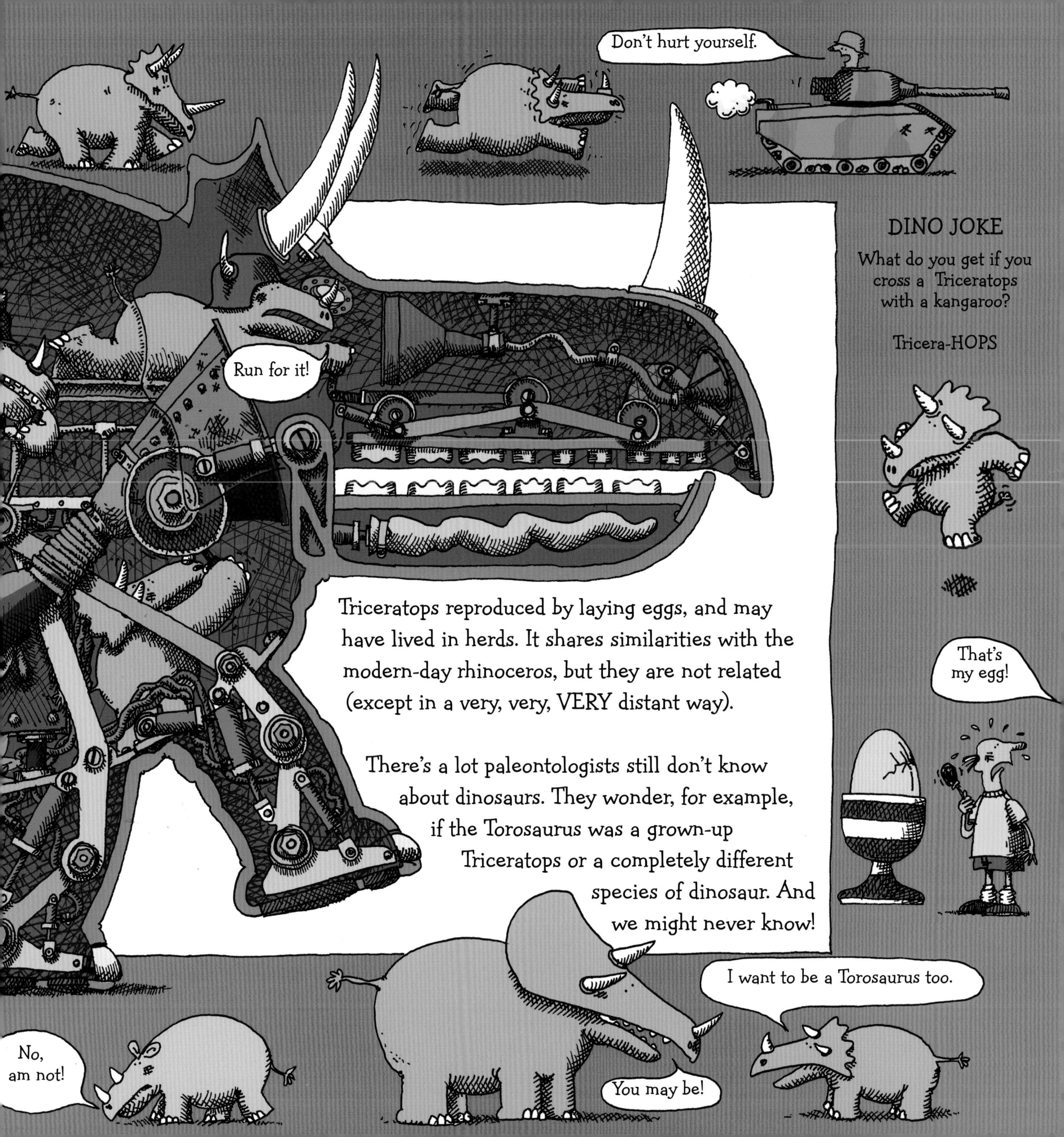

APATOSAURUS (ah-PAT-uh-SAWR-us)
aka BRONTOSAURUS

Apatosaurus means DECEPTIVE LIZARD.

Apatosaurus is more commonly known as the Brontosaurus and existed about 150 million years ago. It is one of the largest land animals that has ever lived—but it wasn't as big as its lesser-known relative, the Supersaurus, which was as long as four buses! The longest Apatosaurus was only as long as two buses but weighed as much as three or four elephants.

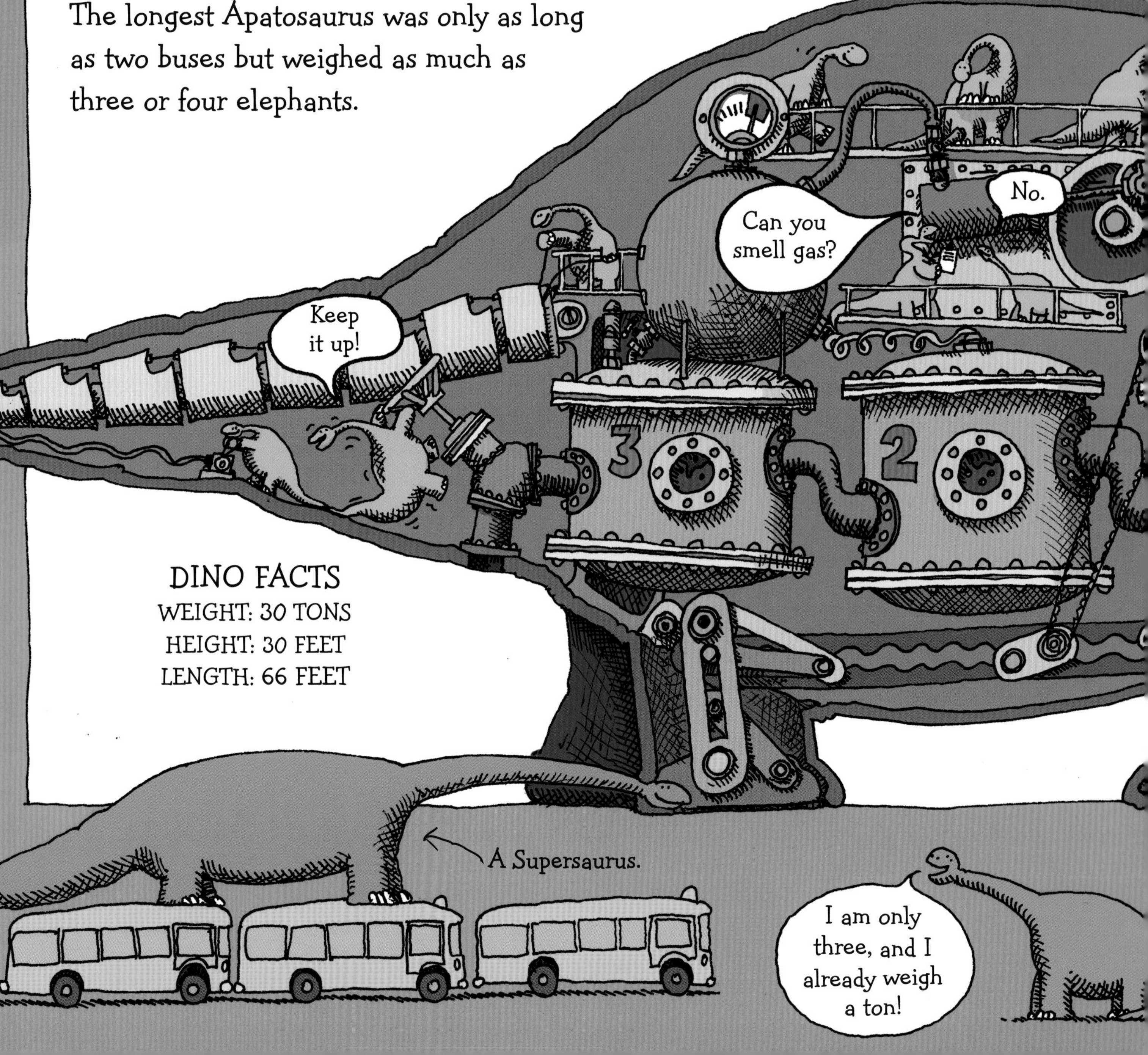

Can you smell gas?

No.

Keep it up!

Typical, you wait for ages and all four come at once.

DINO FACTS
WEIGHT: 30 TONS
HEIGHT: 30 FEET
LENGTH: 66 FEET

A Supersaurus.

I am only three, and I already weigh a ton!

This dinosaur grew incredibly quickly and reached full size by the time it was ten years old. It had an extremely long neck (around twenty feet long) with a rather small head—its brain was probably the size of a big apple! It used its long tail to defend itself. One scientist believes that when Apatosaurus cracked its tail like a whip, it made a noise as loud as a cannon.

DINO JOKE

What's worse than a giraffe with a sore throat?

An Apatosaurus with a sore throat

VELOCIRAPTOR (Veh-loss-ih-RAP-tor)

Velociraptor means RAPID ROBBER.

Velociraptor is one of the most well-known small, predatory dinosaurs. About the size of a turkey, the Velociraptor is nonetheless said to be a cunning and calculating carnivore (meat-eater). It is believed that this dinosaur hunted in groups, not unlike many carnivorous animals today, such as wolves and lions.

Lunch!

DINO FACTS
WEIGHT: 33 POUNDS
HEIGHT: 3 FEET
LENGTH: 7 FEET

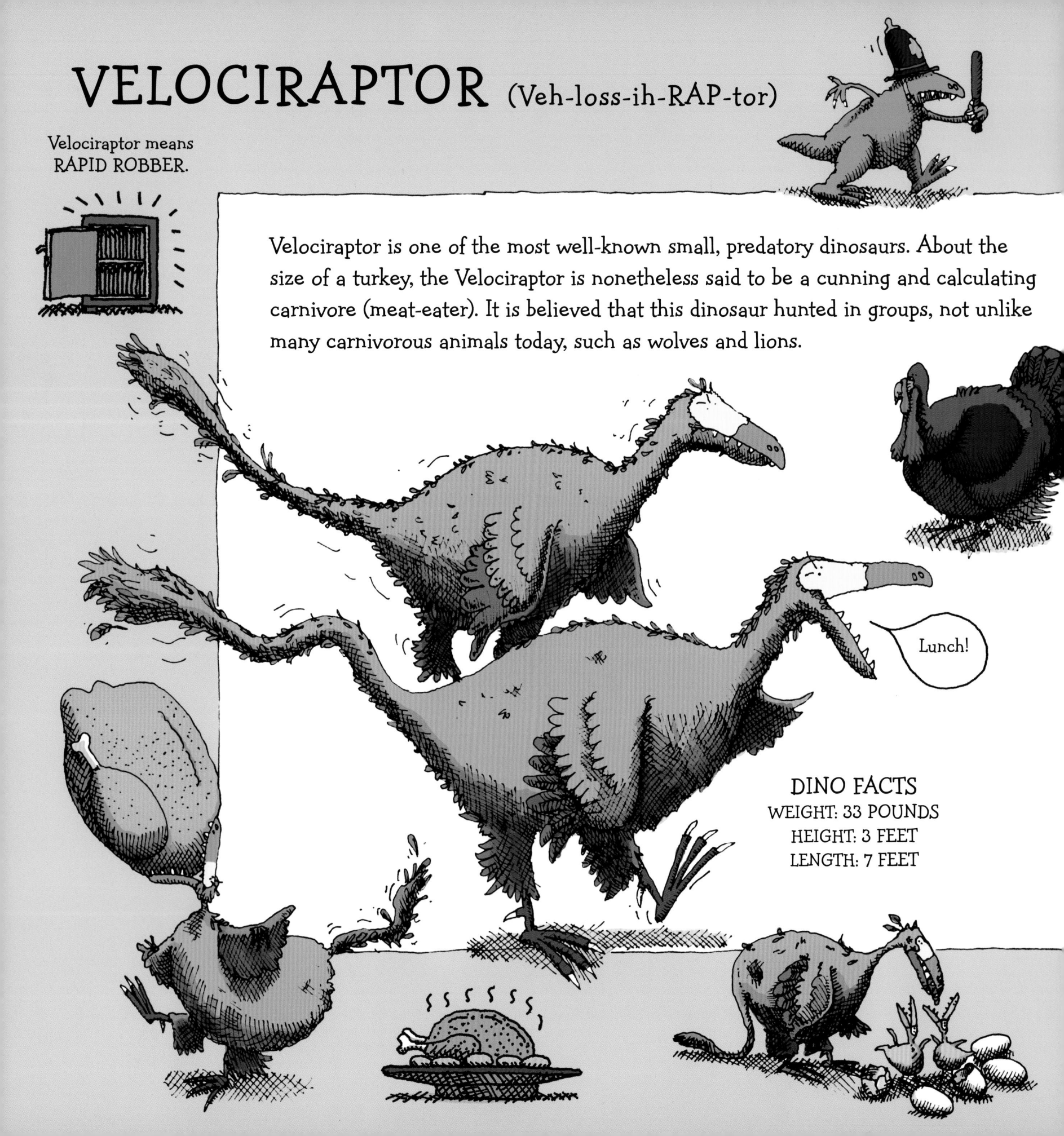

Recently scientists discovered evidence that the Velociraptor may have been feathered. This helps prove the theory that birds descended from dinosaurs, and that feathers actually came first, before the bird's ability to fly.

DINO JOKE

What happened when the dinosaur took the train home?

He had to bring it back!

TYRANNOSAURUS REX

(tye-RAN-uh-SAWR-us)

Tyrannosaurus means TYRANT LIZARD. Rex means KING.

Tyrannosaurus Rex is often known by its nickname: T. rex. It is one of the biggest carnivores that has ever lived and weighed more than four small cars. Its jaws were so strong that it would probably h ave been able to chomp down on a medium-size tree. But it probably wouldn't have ever done so—this dinosaur DEFINITELY preferred tasty meat. It could eat 550 pounds of meat in one bite! It is thought to have lived by hunting and scavenging for dead animals.

T. rex's head was almost seven feet long, but it had very short arms. In fact, its arms were so short that they couldn't even reach its mouth! Some scientists believe that T. rex could run at speeds of forty-five miles per hour (but wasn't nearly as fast when turning corners). The biggest T. rex tooth ever found was bigger than a man's foot!

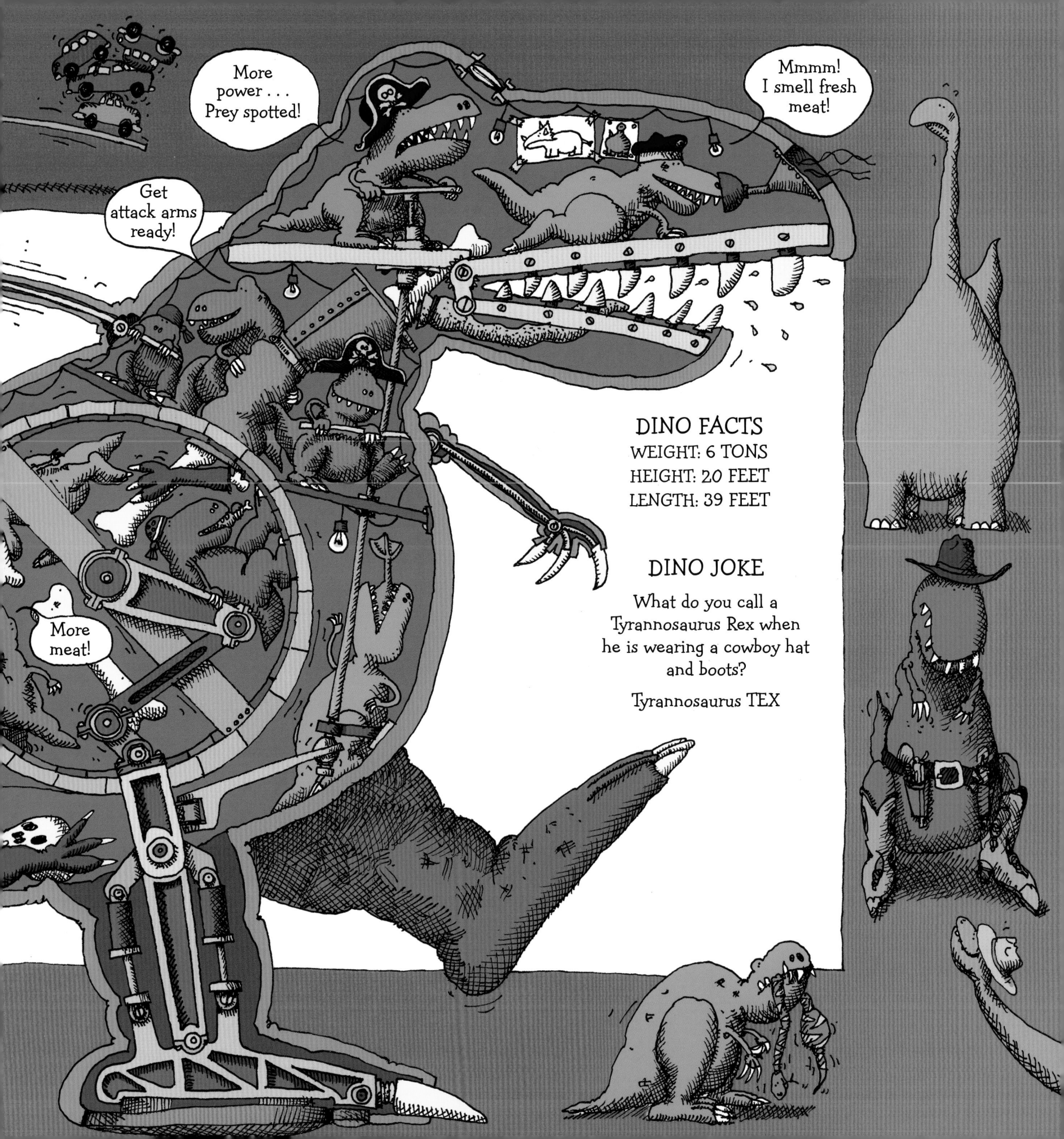

DINO FACTS
WEIGHT: 6 TONS
HEIGHT: 20 FEET
LENGTH: 39 FEET

DINO JOKE

What do you call a Tyrannosaurus Rex when he is wearing a cowboy hat and boots?

Tyrannosaurus TEX

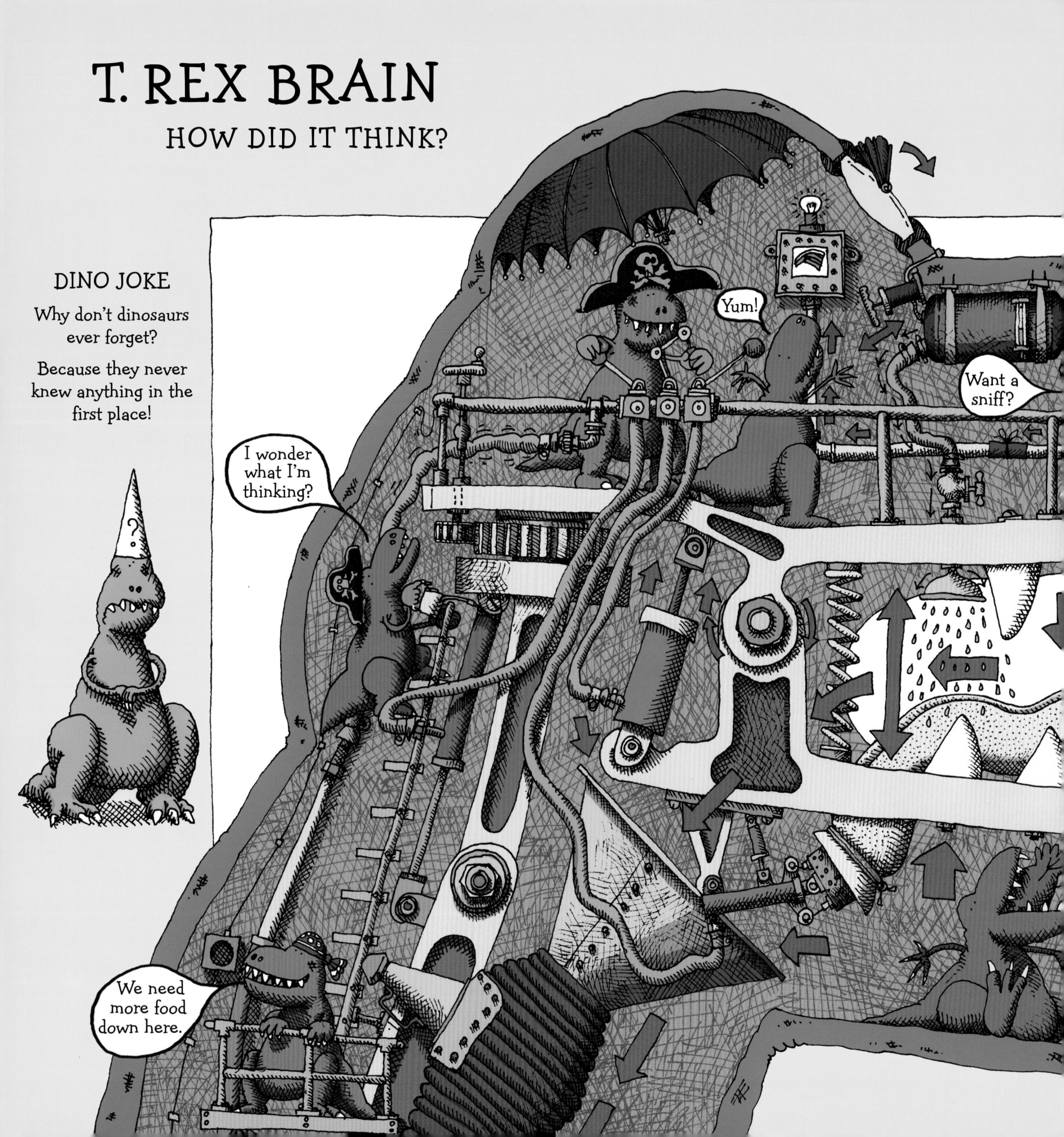

Fig. 1

Fig. 2

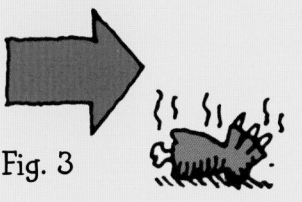

Fig. 3

Fig. 4

Fig. 5

Fig. 6

Fig. 7

T. rex may not have been the cleverest of creatures, but it wasn't the dumbest, either. It had a fantastic sense of smell and could sniff out rotting dead animals from a long way away, and live animals from almost as far. Its brain was bigger than those of most other dinosaurs. It was actually about the same size as a human brain, but the bit that did the thinking was much smaller. Many of its thoughts were very simple and probably went something like this:

1. The smell of rotting meat! Delicious!
2. I need meat!
3. Make body go in that direction!
4. Legs move!
5. Avoid tree!
6. Eyes look for dead thing!
7. Ooh, that looks dead and the smell is really nifty.
8. Open jaws.
9. Bend down.
10. Chomp!
11. YUM!

Fig. 11

Fig. 10

Fig. 9

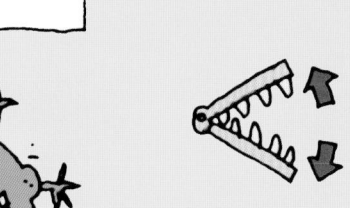

Fig. 8

WEIRD AND WONDERFUL DINOSAURS

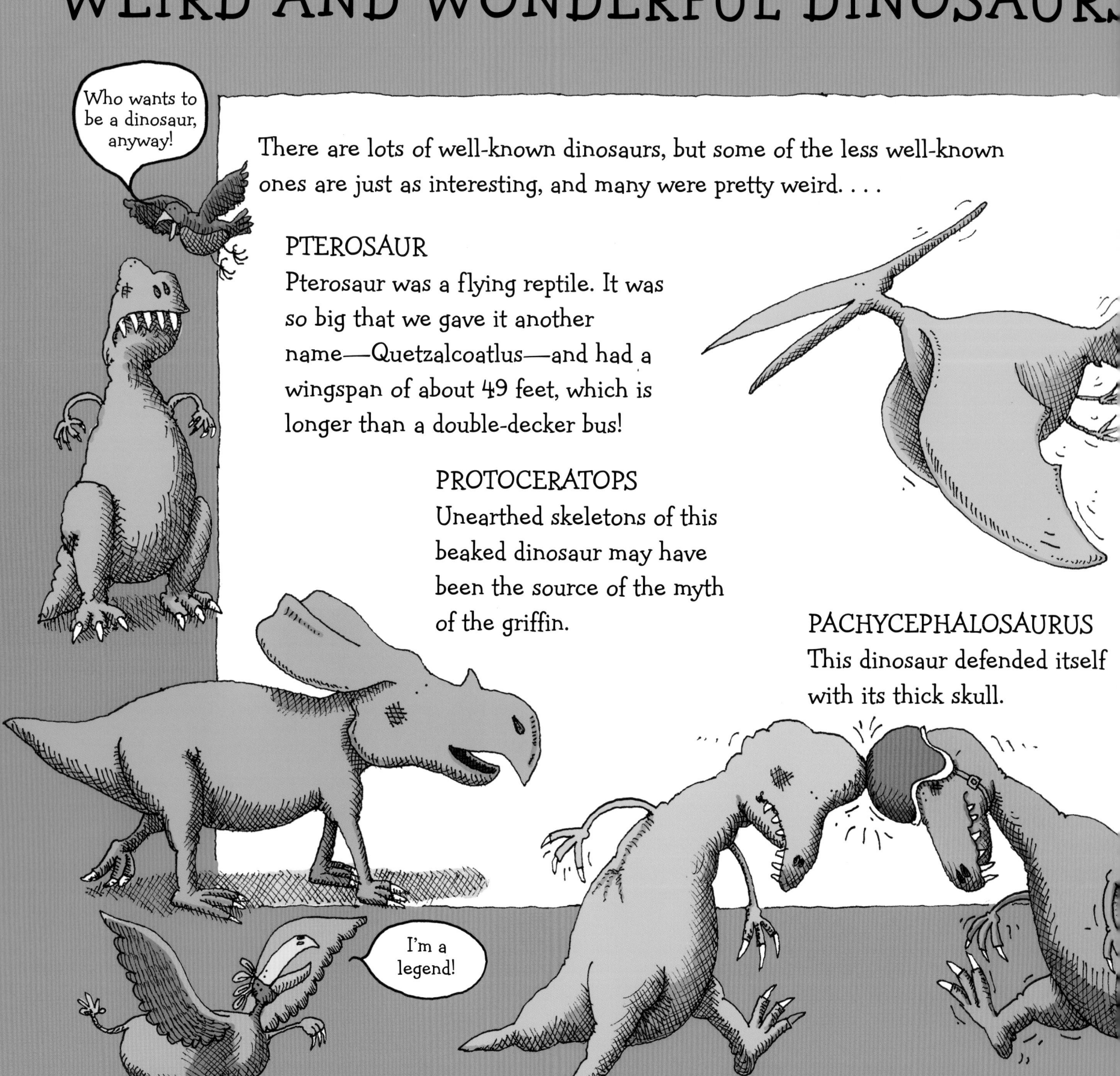

Who wants to be a dinosaur, anyway!

There are lots of well-known dinosaurs, but some of the less well-known ones are just as interesting, and many were pretty weird. . . .

PTEROSAUR
Pterosaur was a flying reptile. It was so big that we gave it another name—Quetzalcoatlus—and had a wingspan of about 49 feet, which is longer than a double-decker bus!

PROTOCERATOPS
Unearthed skeletons of this beaked dinosaur may have been the source of the myth of the griffin.

PACHYCEPHALOSAURUS
This dinosaur defended itself with its thick skull.

I'm a legend!

THERIZINOSAURUS
This vegetarian dinosaur had huge claws that were about three feet in length.

CARNOTAURUS
This dinosaur had arms so short they were little more than stumps.

JEHOLOPTERUS
It was once thought that this small, hairy pterosaur may have attached itself to large dinosaurs and sucked their blood—a prehistoric vampire!

TSINTAOSAURUS SPINORHINUS
This dinosaur had a bill like a duck and a horn like a unicorn.

DINO JOKE
What do you call a dinosaur that picks its nose and eats it?

Disgusting!

THE END OF THE DINOSAURS

Where on Earth did they go?

There are many theories as to why dinosaurs died out. Here are some of them:

1. Either a comet hit Earth or a huge volcanic eruption caused such a large cloud of dust in the atmosphere that it completely changed the weather, making it much too hot or cold for their survival.

2. Changes to Earth's temperatures and sea levels destroyed the dinosaurs' habitats.

3. They were infected by new diseases, which were probably carried by insects.

4. New and more successful creatures evolved and the dinosaurs couldn't compete with them.

Someone turn the tap off!

Yum, this is egg-cellent!

Brrr! It's cold.

DINO JOKE

Why did the dinosaur go extinct?

Because it wouldn't take a bath!

DINOSAURS TODAY

DINO JOKE

What do you get if you cross a crocodile with a flower?

I don't know, but I'm not going to smell it!

These creatures lived during the time of the dinosaurs and are still around today.

CROCODILES

Crocodiles are not (and were never) dinosaurs, but they lived at the same time. They were probably not as bright as some dinosaurs—and yet they're the ones still alive today, so they've got *something* going for them!

SHARKS

Sharks first appeared about 400 million years ago, long before the first dinosaurs. Megalodon was the largest shark that ever lived. It was about the same size as a humpback whale, and its jaws were so large it could have swallowed a cow whole!

I love burgers!

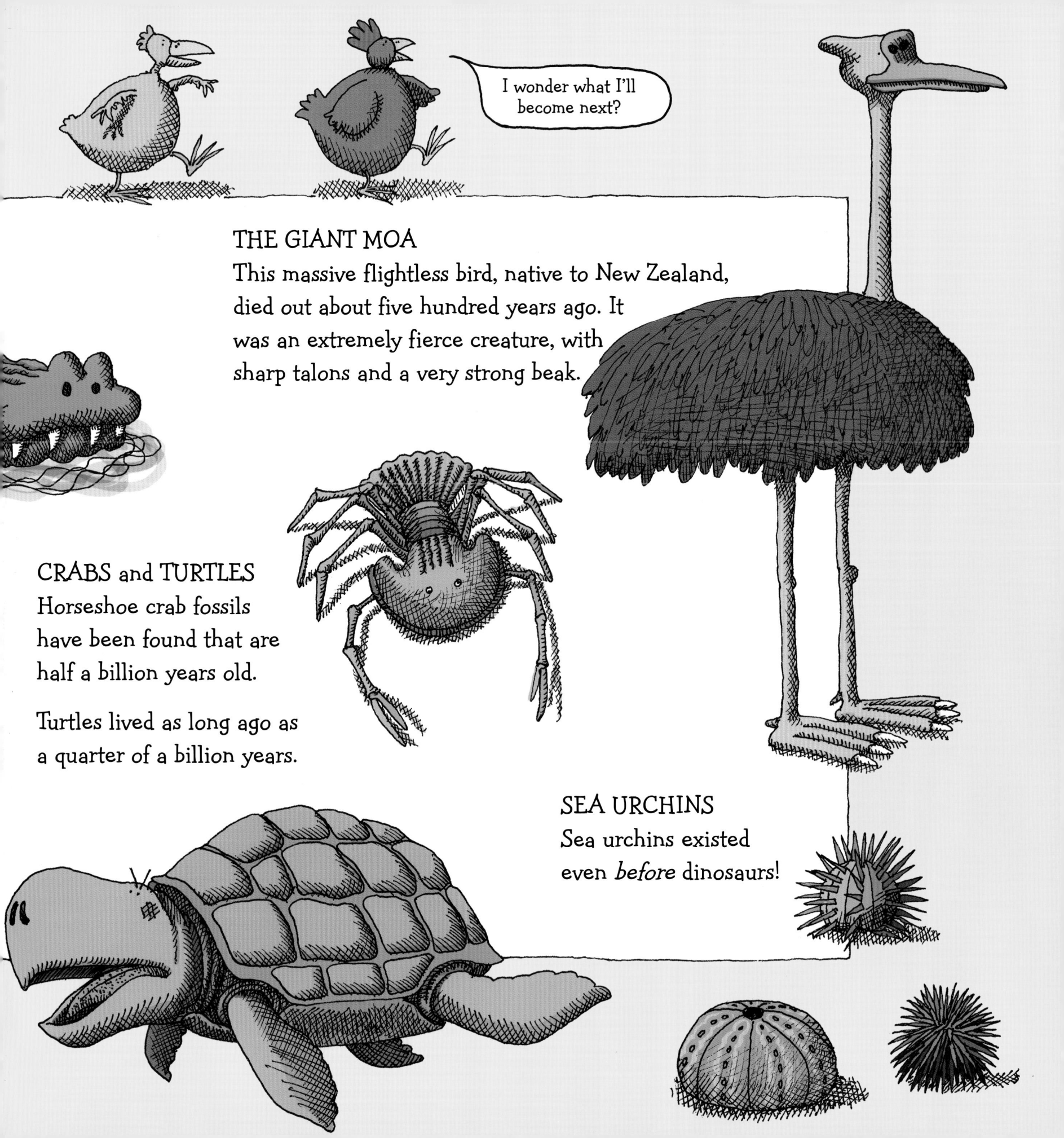

I wonder what I'll become next?

THE GIANT MOA

This massive flightless bird, native to New Zealand, died out about five hundred years ago. It was an extremely fierce creature, with sharp talons and a very strong beak.

CRABS and TURTLES

Horseshoe crab fossils have been found that are half a billion years old.

Turtles lived as long ago as a quarter of a billion years.

SEA URCHINS

Sea urchins existed even *before* dinosaurs!

HOW TO BUILD A WOOLLY MAMMOTH

(Please note: not a dinosaur)

The Woolly Mammoth was a distant relation of the elephant. A mammal, and not actually a dinosaur, it first appeared about one million years ago and died out around three and a half thousand years ago (long after the invention of root beer and ice skating!). They are often found frozen in ice in Siberia.

Three layers of hair to keep the cold out

Small ears so as not to lose heat through them

To make a Woolly Mammoth, you might do the following:

- Get one full-size Asian elephant
- Wrap it in enough padding to keep out the bitter Arctic cold
- Extend its tusks
- Hide buns under the snow for it to find and eat
- Try and keep the Woolly Mammouth happy!

MAMMOTH JOKE

Why did the Woolly Mammoth cross the road?

Because there were no chickens in the Ice Age.